Lizzie McGuire MYSTERIES

GET A CLUE!

By Lisa Banim
Based on the series
created by Terri Minsky

Watch it on
Disney CHANNEL   abc Kids

Disney PRESS

New York

Printed in the United States of America

First Edition
1 3 5 7 9 10 8 6 4 2

Library of Congress Catalog Card Number: 2003112332

ISBN 0-7868-4620-8
For more Disney Press fun, visit www.disneybooks.com
Visit DisneyChannel.com

1

To Lizzie McGuire, solving a mystery was a lot like trying to get through junior high.

No matter where she went, suspicious types were whispering behind her back. Someone—usually the principal—was trying to discover the identity of a "guilty party." And most of the time, she felt totally clueless.

So, weirdly enough, on the day a *real* mystery got dropped on Lizzie's head, she was actually sort of ready for it.

The morning itself started out like any other

totally typical school day. Lizzie was walking toward her first class when her best friend Miranda Sanchez called, "Lizzie, heads up! Ethan alert at nine o'clock!"

"Really?" Lizzie turned so quickly, her long blond hair hit Miranda in the face.

Show yourself, crush-boy! A smile from you can make my week—let alone my day!

But the hottest hottie at Hillridge Junior High was nowhere in sight.

"I don't see Ethan," said Lizzie. "Where is he?"

"*Um*, actually, he's nowhere," Miranda admitted, after spitting Lizzie's hair out of her mouth. "I just wanted to make sure you were awake. We have our first class with the new English teacher today."

"Gee, thanks," said Lizzie sarcastically.

Miranda was the sort of friend who kept you on your toes. Unfortunately, Lizzie wasn't always in the mood to make like a prima ballerina.

With a sigh, Lizzie adjusted her heavy knapsack and continued down the crowded hallway.

"I can't believe you two make such a big deal over Ethan Craft," complained Gordo, Lizzie's other best friend. "I mean, he's just a *guy*."

Lizzie and Miranda rolled their eyes.

"*Uh*, right, Gordo," Lizzie said.

Gordo, aka David Gordon, was a guy himself. So, of course, he wouldn't understand. Trying to explain why she and Miranda were crushin' on Ethan would be like trying to explain why ice cream tasted good. It was just . . . beyond words.

The bell rang as they reached their classroom. A tall woman in a tweed jacket clapped her hands. She was their new English teacher.

"Hurry, hurry, people," she said. "We have a lot to do today."

Most of the other kids were already in their seats. Lizzie, Miranda, and Gordo tried to find three desks together. No luck.

Lizzie headed for a seat at the back of the room. On her way, she nearly tripped over Kate Sanders's new, expensive-looking sling-back heels.

"Watch it, McGuire," Kate said.

Kate was sitting with Claire and some of her other cheerleader friends. They all looked totally put together, as usual. Coordinated outfits with diamond earrings and either pearl or slinky gold necklaces. Teeth whitened, nails done, hair totally perfect.

Not that Lizzie looked like a slouch. She'd dressed in a cool outfit this morning herself— blue-and-white-print capri pants, a cute baby tee with a yellow sunburst, and her yellow platforms. She'd used the "magic hair" thingy to part her hair with a cool zigzag design. And for jewelry she'd worn her heart necklace and multicolored bangle bracelets.

"Um, whatever," Lizzie mumbled to Kate. Then she slid into her seat.

Sometimes Lizzie couldn't believe she and Kate had ever been friends. But that was way back in grade school. Kate was superpopular now. And supersnobby.

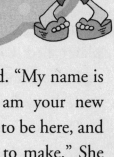

Kate's the worse kind of she-beast—she doesn't just make you *feel* invisible. She makes you wish you *were* invisible!

"So, everyone," the teacher said. "My name is Ms. Philomena George, and I am your new English teacher. I am very excited to be here, and I have a very big announcement to make." She paused dramatically.

Miranda looked back at Lizzie and rolled her eyes. Lizzie shrugged.

Gordo, meanwhile, appeared totally interested. Being a superexcellent, straight-A-plus student, he always paid close attention in class.

Lizzie sat up straight and tried to look interested, too. Okay, so she wasn't a superexcellent, straight-A-plus student, like Gordo. But her grades were pretty good. And she paid attention *most* of the time—when she wasn't being distracted by . . . other things.

She shot a glance at Ethan. He was twirling and retwirling a rubber band around his fingers.

"We will embark on a thrilling adventure in your genre studies," Ms. George said, "in a lesson plan called 'Unlocking the Key to the Mystery.'"

Lizzie glanced around the classroom. Nobody *looked* very thrilled.

"And we will begin by writing our very own mystery stories," Ms. George went on. "Your first drafts are due next Monday."

Everyone groaned loudly.

Yikes, Lizzie thought. That's only a week away.

"But here is the most exciting part," Ms. George said. "Valerie King, the editor of *Chief Suspect* magazine, is a good friend of mine. I will submit our best story to be published in her new spin-off magazine, *Chief Suspect Junior*!"

"Uh, chief *what*?" Ethan asked.

A redheaded girl named Carole with braids, braces, and glasses sat up straight in her seat and raised her hand. She'd moved to Hillridge a few weeks before, and she kept mostly to herself.

"Everyone who's *anyone* in the mystery world knows *Chief Suspect* magazine," Carole said. "My mother was interviewed for the first issue. She's an expert in the mystery field."

Ms. George beamed. "I saw that interview! It was very interesting. So you're Samantha Shelton's daughter?"

Carole nodded proudly.

"Well, I'm sure the class would love to hear more about your mother sometime," said Ms. George.

Carole nodded again.

Lizzie knew that Samantha Shelton was Carole's mother, but she'd never heard Carole speak in class before today. Having an author for a mom sounded pretty cool to Lizzie. Of course, not everyone cared.

Lizzie glanced at Kate and Claire. They were discussing their manicures.

Ms. George picked up the class roster. "So tell me, class," she said. "Have any of you ever solved a real-life mystery?"

No one answered.

Lizzie sneaked another peek at Ethan. He was tying a knot in his rubber band now.

"Oh, dear," Ms. George said. "Surely *someone* has a story to tell us." She glanced down the list of student names. "Miranda Sanchez? How about you?"

Miranda looked startled. Everyone stared at her. "Um, n-no, not me," she stammered. Then she froze, like she'd just remembered something.

"But my best friend Lizzie McGuire solved a mystery once."

Lizzie snapped to attention. *Huh?*

"Wonderful!" Ms. George said. She consulted her student roster again. "And Lizzie is in this class! Where are you, Lizzie McGuire?"

Uh-oh. Lizzie gave a tiny wave and sank as low as she could in her seat. She had solved only one mystery in her whole life. But Miranda wasn't going to tell *that* story. She *couldn't.*

"Tell us all about it, Lizzie," Ms. George said.

A thousand Ping-Pong balls began bouncing around in Lizzie's stomach. "Uh . . . well . . . um . . ."

C'mon! Make up something! Tell her the plot of that cat-who-solves-crimes book you read last week—and just pretend *you're* the cat!

"Well, I . . . uh . . ."

Lizzie saw Gordo cover his face with his hands. How could Miranda have done this to her?!

"It was back in grade school," Miranda spoke up quickly. "Kate Sanders had this really cute teddy bear named Mr. Stewart Wugglesby."

A few kids snickered. Claire, Kate's best friend, actually snorted. Kate shot Claire a murderous look, then turned the look on Lizzie.

Oh, no. Kate thinks i put Miranda up to this. This can't be happening. i'm innocent! i want a lawyer!

"Mr. Wugglesby disappeared," Miranda rushed on. She was really warming up to the story now. "And Kate was *sooo* upset. She *begged* Lizzie to help her find him."

Lizzie heard Kate give a disgusted sigh. Her long, slow breath sounded like a snake hissing. A *poisonous* snake, thought Lizzie.

Am i blushing? Or is that intense burning on my face from the evil laser-stare Kate is zapping at me?

"Anyway, Lizzie had been reading Nancy Drew books all summer," Miranda said. "Like, zillions of them. So she came up with a whole bunch of clues and solved the mystery."

"So, Mr. Stewart Wugglesby was found?" Ms. George asked, smiling.

"Well, yeah," Miranda said. "But he was pretty messed up. Lizzie's little brother had buried him in a sandbox, and then it rained for days and—"

Lizzie pulled her headband down over her

ears. She just couldn't listen to any more. Ring, bell, she thought. *Ring!*

Months seemed to pass before English class finally ended. Lizzie was so mortified, she couldn't even look up until everyone had left the room. Everyone but Miranda and Gordo, of course. They stood waiting for her.

"Ready to go?" Gordo asked. He had a look of pity on his face. It was the sort of look you'd give to a girl on her way to the Arctic without a coat. A "nice knowing you" look.

"Hey, good thing I remembered that teddy-bear thing, *huh*?" Miranda said. "Bet you forgot all about it."

"I wish," Lizzie said.

If only everyone else would forget about it, too. Especially Kate.

2

At lunch, Lizzie stirred her yogurt over and over. She'd been giving Miranda grief all morning.

"I mean it, Miranda. I can't believe you told that stupid teddy-bear story in class!" she cried.

Miranda bit her lip. "Lizzie, chill, already! I said I was sorry. I didn't think it was such a big deal. I just kind of got carried away."

"I know," Lizzie said. "And I know you didn't know what you were doing. I'm just really worried. Kate looked so totally embarrassed. I don't know what she's gonna—"

Lizzie cut off her words with a strangled squeak. Lunch tray in hand, Kate had stopped dead, right in front of Lizzie's table. Slowly, she leaned down.

"McGuire," Kate said loudly. "You and your little friend are going to be . . . So. Unbelievably. Sorry." Then she turned and stormed off toward the cheerleaders' table.

"Whatever," said Miranda.

"No," said Lizzie. "This is not a *whatever.* This is a *what next?!*"

"Lizzie, don't pay any attention to Kate," Gordo advised. "She's just trying to bug you."

"Well, she's doing a good job!" Lizzie cried.

Miranda coolly peeled a banana. "You know what I think?" she said. "I think Kate's never gotten over Lizzie beating her in that fifth-grade summer reading contest."

Gordo raised one eyebrow. "Reading contest?"

"Yeah," Miranda answered. "Don't you remember? Lizzie topped Kate by reading every

Nancy Drew book *plus* one Hardy Boys to win. You remember, Lizzie, don't you?"

Lizzie nodded. "Yep. It *was* a major moment."

YES! YES! V-i-C-T-O-R-Y!
Hey, when you lose your class presidential election to a guy whose campaign slogan is "i'll eat a worm for every vote," you learn to cherish *any* memory of victory you've got!

Someone tapped Lizzie's arm. "Excuse me," said a timid voice.

Lizzie looked over her shoulder. It was Carole Shelton from English class. She'd turned around in her seat at the lunch table right behind them.

"Sorry, I didn't mean to eavesdrop," Carole

said. "But did you really read every single Nancy Drew book?"

Lizzie nodded. "It's true. I'm a major fan."

"Me, too," Carole said. "Nancy Drew is so cool. I want to be just like her."

"Totally," Lizzie agreed.

"My mom is a mystery writer," Carole said, biting her nails.

"We know," Gordo said. "You already told us about it in class."

Carole blushed. "Oh," she said. She stopped biting her nails and nervously twirled one of her red braids as she gazed at Gordo. "Right. Sorry, I forgot."

"Hey, your mom sounds really cool," Gordo added quickly.

"Thanks. She is," Carole said. Then she gave Gordo a little smile.

Lizzie's eyebrows rose. That smile of Carole's looked a little flirty. Well, well, well, thought Lizzie, could Gordo have a female fan?

Jealous? Me? As if!

Just as Carole turned away from Lizzie's table, another visitor stopped by—Ms. Young, the assistant guidance counselor. She was a thin, pale woman with wild-looking brown hair and tortoiseshell glasses. She had just started working at the school.

"Hello, hello, hello!" Ms. Young greeted them brightly. "Are we all enjoying our lunch?"

"Yes," Gordo answered. "We are."

Lizzie and Miranda shrugged and nodded.

"Wonderful!" Ms. Young gushed. "It's very important that young people get a break during the busy school day. And eat a healthy, nutrient-rich meal as well."

"Right," Lizzie said. She held up her carton of yogurt.

"I just wanted to let you all know that my office

is *always* open," Ms. Young continued. "If you ever need to talk about anything. Or feel you're under any kind of *pressure*."

Pressure? in this junior-high jungle? Where heinous she-beasts plot your downfall on a daily basis . . . ? Nah!

Lizzie, Miranda, and Gordo just smiled and nodded at Ms. Young.

"Well, see you kids later," said the assistant counselor. Then she zoomed off toward another table. "Remember: *anytime!*"

Miranda stared after the woman and said, "That was kinda weird."

"Yeah," said Lizzie. "Ms. Young's kinda . . ."

"Intense," said Gordo.

"Yeah," Miranda agreed. "It's like she's going from table to table, *looking* for someone who needs her help."

"Well, none of us has cracked up yet," said Lizzie.

"*Yet* being the crucial word," said Gordo.

There wasn't much lunchtime left. Lizzie finished her yogurt. Gordo started talking about an old horror movie he'd watched on cable the night before—*Frankenstein* or *The Mummy* or something—and Lizzie felt herself spacing out.

Things are just fine, Lizzie told herself, hardly noticing the dozens of students and teachers filing by her table on their way out of the lunchroom.

I'm sitting here with my two best friends. And Kate hasn't actually killed me for humiliating her in front of our whole English class . . . yet.

Ahem! Like Gordo said, "*Yet* being the crucial word."

By the time the bell rang, Lizzie was feeling pretty good. The whole Mr. Stewart Wugglesby deal wasn't so terrible, really. Kids probably even thought the idea of Kate Sanders's having a fuzzy-wuzzy teddy was cute.

But as Lizzie, Miranda, and Gordo were leaving the cafeteria, Gordo pointed to the books Lizzie was carrying. "Hey, what's that?" he asked.

Lizzie glanced down. A square yellow note was stuck on her English notebook.

"No clue," Lizzie said, peeling off the little slip of paper.

Miranda looked over Lizzie's shoulder. "It's some kind of note," she said.

Lizzie frowned. Two words were scrawled across the yellow square in big purple letters:

McGUIRE, BEWARE!

CHAPTER

3

Lizzie stared down at the message in horror. "Beware?" she repeated. "Beware of *what*?"

"Beware of nothing," Gordo said. "It's obviously someone's idea of a joke."

"A sick joke," Miranda pointed out.

Gordo shrugged. "It's just a yellow sticky note. It could have been stuck anywhere. By anyone. On anyone. You know, like a KICK ME sign on your back."

Lizzie was still looking at the note, frowning.

"But it has my name on it," she pointed out. "See? *McGuire*."

Miranda and Gordo gave each other uneasy glances.

"Lizzie does have a point there," Miranda admitted.

"I *still* say it's bogus," Gordo said. "Come on, we're going to be late for math. I heard Word-problem Wortman is plotting a pop quiz."

But Lizzie didn't move. "You know," she said slowly. "Only one person calls me *McGuire*."

"Kate," Miranda and Gordo said together.

Lizzie sighed and leaned against the wall next to the water fountain. "I knew it! She really *is* out to get me."

Gordo cleared his throat. "*Uh*, Lizzie, don't you think maybe you're blowing this whole Kate thing just a *tiny bit* out of proportion?"

"No," Lizzie said stubbornly. "The girl hates my guts. Especially now."

"Another good point," said Miranda.

Gordo ran a hand through his curly dark hair. He was obviously trying to stay cool. "Okay, let's look at this calmly, logically—"

You want logic? i'll give you logic! i. Am. Kate-bait!

"It's pretty simple, Gordo," Lizzie said. "Didn't you hear what Kate said to me back in the cafeteria?"

"I did," Miranda said helpfully. "She said you'd be sorry. *Unbelievably* sorry."

"Thanks, Miranda," Lizzie said.

Miranda nodded. "You're welcome."

Gordo seemed really frustrated now. "Look," he said, "Kate may be pretty scary sometimes. I'll grant you that. But she's hardly *dangerous*. In the criminal sense, anyway. Okay? You have to admit *that*."

This time, Gordo had scored a point.

Maybe I *am* overreacting, Lizzie told herself. Just a little. "Okay," she said in a small voice.

"Okay," Miranda echoed.

Gordo looked pleased. "Glad to be of service," he said. He took both girls by their T-shirt sleeves and began guiding them down the hall. "Now it's time for a pop quiz!"

"You don't have to sound so cheery about it," Miranda grumbled.

But Lizzie wasn't thinking about the horrors of a surprise math test. Or the fact that she hadn't actually finished her math homework last night.

She was thinking about the warning.

Lizzie had to admit, Gordo was usually right about things. Word-problem Wortman started handing out those pop quizzes almost as soon as they'd sat down.

"Twenty problems, twenty minutes," the teacher said. "That should give all of you who completed last night's homework assignment *plenty* of time."

"Yikes!" Miranda mouthed to Lizzie.

Lizzie threw her friend a helpless look. Then she reached into the open side pocket of her knapsack to get a pencil.

No luck.

She'd have to use her favorite purple pen. It was a felt-tip, so it wouldn't erase. Oh, well, Lizzie told herself. Guess I should stick with my first guess, anyway.

But the purple pen wasn't in the side pocket of her knapsack, either.

i've been robbed! i've been robbed! Um, excuse me, Mrs. Wortman? Under the circumstances, i don't feel i should have to take this quiz.

All the kids around Lizzie had already started the test. Now, she had nineteen minutes.

Trying not to panic, Lizzie checked her knapsack one more time. All she found was the creepy yellow note she had stuffed inside the pocket as she had walked into class.

McGUIRE, BEWARE! stared up at her in a line of nasty purple squiggles.

Whoa. Purple? *Waitie* just a sec!

Whoever wrote that message used *my* pen, Lizzie realized. I had it right with me when I was in the cafeteria.

And *who* had been in the cafeteria, close enough to steal her pen right out from under her nose?

Across the room, Kate gave a loud, fake cough. When Lizzie glanced at her, Kate narrowed her eyes and gave Lizzie one of her trademark poisonous stares.

Lizzie gulped.

"Fifteen minutes, ladies and gentlemen," Mrs.

Wortman announced. "Ms. Sanders, do you need to use the water fountain?"

"No, thank you," Kate said sweetly. Then she looked back down at her test.

Lizzie finally broke down, raised her hand, and asked the teacher to lend her a pencil. Then she spent the next fourteen minutes trying to solve the mystery of quadratic equations.

"Time!" Mrs. Wortman called loudly. "All papers to the front of the room, please."

Hey, who needs algebra when you'll probably never even make it out of junior high?

For the rest of the day, Lizzie tried to avoid Kate as much as possible. It wasn't easy. The cheer queen seemed to pop up everywhere.

On her way to art class, Lizzie walked straight

into a trash container when she spotted Kate all the way down the hall.

After art, Lizzie saw Kate again and almost tripped Gordo as she tried to duck into a corner. Then she banged her head on a fire extinguisher.

Finally, the last bell rang.

Can this day get any worse? Lizzie thought as she headed to her locker. She felt totally exhausted.

Hannah Marvin, the girl who had the locker next to Lizzie's, was already packing up her stuff to go home.

"Hi, Lizzie," said Hannah. "Hey, I heard about your finding Kate's teddy bear. That was *soooo* sweet."

"Yeah," Lizzie said, fumbling with her combination. "Sweet."

Suddenly, Hannah gasped. "What's this?" she said.

Lizzie looked up. "What's what?" she asked.

Hannah was looking at her really funny. Her face was so white, her freckles stood out like a Dalmatian's spots. And she was holding something behind her back.

"Um, Hannah?" Lizzie prodded. "Is everything okay?"

"Oh, sure," Hannah said. "Just fine." But she took off at a run down the hall, leaving her locker door open.

What's up with *that?* Lizzie wondered. She started to follow Hannah.

But then, Lizzie saw the girl toss something into the trash as she charged out the door. Something *yellow.*

"Uh-oh," Lizzie murmured, remembering the note that she herself had gotten earlier in the day.

Lizzie hurried toward the trash can and peered inside. Sure enough, there was a square yellow note sitting on top of all the garbage. And the note had *purple* writing on it.

Lizzie glanced both ways to make sure no one was spying on her. Then she reached into the trash and plucked out the note. It read:

I KNOW WHAT YOU DID
LAST WEEK. . . .

But that wasn't the worst part. This time, there were two big, purple initials at the end of the message.

—L.M.

Huh? Lizzie thought. L.M.? I don't know any L.M.'s.

Except one.

Me!

*O*hmigosh, thought Lizzie, what's worse? Getting a creepy note myself? Or finding someone else's note—*signed* by me?

Lizzie almost dropped the yellow note straight back in the trash. Then she changed her mind. She stuffed it into her knapsack, next to the first one.

Evidence, she told herself. Just in case.

The person who wrote Hannah's note is definitely trying to make me, Lizzie McGuire, look

bad, she thought. It has to be Kate, of course.
Or . . . maybe not.

Mean notes aren't really Kate's style. She's more seriously up-front about her meanness. When she's nasty, she's nasty right to your *face*.

Anyway, thought Lizzie, why would Kate want to scare Hannah? She wasn't a member of the superpopular crowd, but she wasn't a she-geek, either. Like Lizzie herself, Hannah was just a typical part of the student population—what Gordo called "the normals."

Lizzie walked through the exit doors, puzzling about it. Then, for a nanosecond, Lizzie wondered what terrible thing Hannah could have done last week. The note made it sound like something pretty terrible. But still—*Hannah?*

I'll just have to explain to her that I didn't send

the note, Lizzie thought. Hannah will understand. No big.

I hope.

Lizzie headed toward the line of buses in the
school parking lot. She kept looking around. She
didn't want to risk running into Kate on the way
home. Especially today.

Neither Miranda nor Gordo was going home
with Lizzie today. Miranda had band practice.
And Gordo was staying after school to work on
some project with Larry Tudgeman for Science
Club.

Lizzie got on the bus and flopped back in her
seat. But she couldn't shake those yellow notes
out of her mind.

Should she just go up to Kate and accuse her
of writing them? Kate would probably laugh in
her face.

And what if Kate hadn't written them?

I'll just have to find out, Lizzie decided. One
thing was certain: the creepy notes had to stop. It

was time to put on her sleuthing hat and get to the bottom of this.

I just hope this sleuthing hat doesn't give me hat hair!

Lizzie's day didn't improve a whole lot after she got home. Her annoying little brother, Matt, and his buddy Lanny were glued to their new fave TV show, *Detective Dude*.

"Do you have to watch that right now?" Lizzie asked as she walked into the living room. She picked up the remote from the coffee table.

"*Excuuuuse me!*" Matt said. He grabbed back the remote. "It's three o'clock. Prime time for crime with *Detective Dude*."

Lanny nodded eagerly. The kid didn't talk much. In fact, Lizzie had never actually heard him say one word. Only Matt seemed to know what Lanny was thinking—like he was Lanny's official translator.

"*Detective Dude* is totally lame," Lizzie complained. She dropped down on the couch next to the boys. "I mean, look at him. He's a big, floppy, green *bunny*."

"Rabbit," Matt corrected. He turned to Lanny, who shook his head. "And Lanny says the color is *chartreuse*."

Lizzie threw up her hands. "Whatever!"

"Detective Dude can solve *any* mystery, *any* time," said Matt. "And I can, too. Especially after I get my cool new *Detective Dude* crime-solving kit. I just sent away for it on the Internet. Overnight delivery."

Lizzie raised one eyebrow. Detective kit? He had to be kidding. On the other hand . . .

"All I need is the *perrrrfect* crime to work with," said Matt. "Do you know of any cases that could use my amazing detective skills?"

"NO!" Lizzie said loudly. She hugged a couch pillow to her chest and frowned at the TV.

Here's a mystery you can solve: why are you such a spiky-haired pest?

"She's a little touchy," Matt told Lanny. "Probably hiding something."

Lizzie wanted to throw the pillow at her brother. But starting a fight and getting grounded just didn't seem worth the hassle. She had more important things to deal with right now.

Suddenly, the front door swung open.

"Lizzie!" cried Miranda, running in. "You've got to see this!"

"See what?" Lizzie said, jumping up.

"Yeah, what?" Matt echoed. He bounced off the couch, too.

Lizzie pushed her brother back down. "Watch

your silly crime-solving bunny show," she told him. Then she took Miranda into the kitchen so they could talk privately.

"Where's your mom?" Miranda asked, looking around.

"Visiting Mrs. Henderson down the street," Lizzie said. "But, look—fresh-baked chocolate-chip cookies!" She helped herself to a warm one from a plate on the counter. "Want some?"

"No, thanks," Miranda said.

"You're kidding," Lizzie said in surprise. Miranda loved her mom's cookies.

Miranda put her violin case down on the counter. "Check this out," she said. She reached into the pocket of her jeans. "Once you read it, you'll lose your appetite, too."

Lizzie stopped chewing. "Don't tell me," she said, garbling her words around the half-eaten cookie. "A note."

Miranda nodded. "Yep. And you're not going to like it, either."

"Is it signed by me?" Lizzie asked, quickly gulping down the rest of the cookie.

"*Huh?*" Miranda said. "Signed by *you?*"

Lizzie nodded.

"No," said Miranda as she pulled out the message. It was written on a yellow sticky note with purple ink—just like the other two notes had been. "But look what it says."

Lizzie went over to Miranda and read the note:

EVEN BEST FRIENDS CAN'T BE TRUSTED.

"I found it in my violin case after band practice," Miranda said.

Lizzie was steaming mad. "I can't believe it!" she said. "My best friend gets a note! Now, this is really getting personal!"

She grabbed two more cookies. She hadn't actually lost her appetite, after all. It seemed anger *increased* her appetite.

Then she got a hold of herself. Cookies weren't the solution to this problem.

"Was *Kate* in the band room?" she asked Miranda.

"Kate? Hanging out with band geeks?" Miranda snorted. "I don't think so."

"Well, did you see anyone sneaking around your violin case?"

"No," Miranda said. "The room gets pretty crowded." She cleared her throat. "Um, Lizzie, is there anything you want to tell me?"

Lizzie frowned. "What's that supposed to mean?"

Miranda pushed a broken piece of cookie across the counter with her finger. "I mean, you're my best friend. I can always trust you, right?"

"Of course you can!" Lizzie cried. "You don't believe what this dumb message says, do you?" She took the yellow note from Miranda and tore it into teeny, tiny pieces. "Someone's obviously on a mission to make me look bad. That must be what the note to me meant, the one that said, 'McGuire, Beware!'"

"This is too weird," Miranda said. "I think I missed something."

Lizzie told Miranda about Hannah's note.

Miranda gave a low whistle. "Yep. You're looking pretty bad, all right." She tapped her chin with one finger. "I wonder what Hannah *did* last week?"

Just then, Lizzie heard a muffled sound at the end of the counter. She ran across the room and shouted, "Boo!"

Matt tumbled onto the kitchen floor. Lanny, who'd also been crouching there, fell on top of him.

"A little detective tip from Mystery Matt," her brother told her from the floor. "Never destroy your evidence."

Lizzie narrowed her eyes. Then she looked down at the pieces of torn-up note in her hands.

She threw them all at Matt. "You sneaky little spy!"

Matt cackled with evil glee as yellow confetti floated over him.

Miranda picked up her violin case. "Lizzie, I'd really like to stay and help you figure all this out. But I have a babysitting job."

"That's okay," Lizzie said. "I can solve this case." She glared at Matt. *"Alone."*

As soon as Miranda left, Lizzie went straight up to her bedroom. She made sure to lock the door. She even double-checked the knob. This was serious sleuthing time now.

She sat down at her desk and took her official detective casebook from her knapsack. It was actually her English notebook, but it would have to do.

First, she needed a suspect list.

Well, that was easy. Lizzie wrote "KATE" at the top of a page in big letters.

Had anyone else around her been acting strangely lately? Stranger than usual, anyway?

Lizzie wasn't sure. So she started another column with "MOTIVE" at the top. Another easy one, Lizzie thought. "MAKE ME LOOK BAD," she wrote under the "motive" column.

But that didn't sound very professional. Hmmm, Lizzie thought. How would a real detective put it?

"REVENGE," she wrote.

Next, Lizzie needed a list of clues. So far, she had three yellow notes with mean messages written in purple ink. Well, actually, she now had *two*. She'd ripped up the third.

Lizzie hated to admit it, but Matt was right. She'd made a big mistake destroying a piece of evidence.

She brought out the two notes she had left. The purple handwriting looked exactly the same.

Waitie just a sec, Lizzie thought. She peered closer. Then she checked back at her detective list. The handwriting looks just like *mine*! she realized.

Well, no mystery there. Kate knew Lizzie's handwriting. They'd learned to write together back in first grade.

Lizzie snapped her notebook shut. "Case closed," she said out loud.

Kate is toast.
Make that toast *crumbs.*

"I have this weird feeling," Lizzie told Miranda and Gordo as they walked toward school the next morning. "Like something really bad is going to happen."

"Lizzie," Gordo said. "You're getting all freaked out over nothing."

"Nothing?" Lizzie cried. "You call going up against Kate Sanders *nothing*?"

"No," Gordo said. "I just think you're being a little . . . overly dramatic."

WHAT?! You're accusing ME of being a drama queen? ME?!

"Call it detective's intuition," Lizzie said. She'd already told her friends about her plan to crack the Case of the Nasty Notes.

She'd stayed awake half the night planning what she'd say to Kate. But the truth was, she couldn't be a hundred percent positive that the Supreme Queen of Mean was guilty.

The whole note-writing deal was . . . so *un*-Kate.

"I wish I had more evidence," Lizzie said. "So far, Kate is my best suspect. Okay, my *only* suspect. But I can't totally *prove* she did it."

"Hey," said Miranda, "in Kate's case, she's guilty until proven innocent."

Lizzie looked around as the three entered the school's grassy quad. "You know," she whispered. "Just about anybody here could be out to get me."

"Yoo-hoo!" a voice called out.

"It's Ms. Young," said Miranda. "Over by the picnic tables."

Lizzie and Gordo turned around. Sure enough, the assistant guidance counselor was sitting on a bench. She smiled and waved at them.

"How's it going, kids?" she called. "Is everything coolie?"

Lizzie cringed. Miranda shut her eyes. Ms. Young was *so* not cool.

"Just fine!" Lizzie called back, with a polite smile.

Gordo shook his head. "One thing you have to say for Ms. Young. She's serious about her job."

"Or maybe seriously *nutty* about doing her job," Miranda muttered.

Just then, Carole came up. She fell into step beside them.

"Hi, Carole," Gordo said. "How's your mom?"

"*Really* busy," Carole answered. "She's on a big deadline for her next book. Her publisher is calling from New York every two minutes."

"Wow," Miranda said.

Carole sighed. "Well, that's what it's like when you're an author." She twirled one of her red braids. "So, how are you guys doing on your stories for English class?"

"Huh?" Lizzie and Miranda said together.

Then Lizzie remembered. *Oops.* She'd been too busy with her detective notes last night to start on the mystery assignment. But she had plenty of time left.

"Oh, I started mine," Gordo said. "It's a spoof of Sir Arthur Conan Doyle's *Hound of the Baskervilles.* That's a Sherlock Holmes mystery," he added quickly.

"Sure," Carole said. She pushed up her glasses and began chewing on her thumbnail. "My mom read them all to me when I was, like, five."

Whoa! She was hearing Sherlock Holmes say, "Elementary, my dear Watson," before she even started elementary school. How can I compete with that?!

"Hey, what's the deal over there?" Miranda asked. She pointed to the other side of the quad.

The cheerleaders, dressed in their blue-and-white uniforms, were arranging and rearranging themselves in a line. Kate was bossing all of them around.

"No, no, NO," Lizzie heard her say. "Marcie,

you're 'Teddy,' so you go on the *end*. Now, MOVE!"

"What are they doing?' Gordo asked, shaking his head. "I've never seen cheerleaders act so confused. Witchy—yes. Confused—no."

"Looks like they have notes," Miranda said.

"Must be learning a new cheer," Lizzie said.

"No, Lizzie. *Notes*," Miranda said. "As in square, yellow sticky notes. Look!"

Lizzie looked again. Sure enough, each of the eight girls—including Kate and her best friend, Claire—were holding little squares of yellow paper.

"Let's walk past them into the building really, really fast," Miranda suggested nervously.

"No," Lizzie said, frowning. "I'm on the case, remember? We have to find out what those notes say." She started toward the group of cheerleaders, her heart pounding.

"Yikes," Miranda said. "Here comes Kate. And she's not looking very *cheer*-y."

Lizzie tried not to freak. Kate was storming over like a blond thundercloud.

"Okay, McGuire," Kate said. She stopped in front of Lizzie and her friends. "Is this your twisted idea of a joke?"

"W-what are you talking about?" Lizzie asked. Her big plan of standing up to Kate burst like a bath bubble.

"We just got here," Gordo pointed out.

"Oh, yeah? Well, then, how do you explain *this*?" Kate asked. She snapped her fingers, and the rest of the cheerleaders ran up behind her. They waved their yellow sticky notes like pom-poms.

"Now I've seen everything," Miranda said under her breath.

"Places," Kate commanded.

Lizzie's mouth dropped open as the cheerleaders hustled into line. Each cheerleader read her note out loud:

TEDDY
MADE KATE
C-R-Y.
NOW SHE NEEDS
TO GET
A LIFE!

Then the last three girls in line yelled:

SIGNED:
LIZZIE McGUIRE!

When the cheer was over, Kate put her hands on her hips and glared at Lizzie. "So, what's up with *that*, McGuire?" she shouted.

Catchy! Good luck at cheer camp.

"Uh . . . um . . ." sputtered Lizzie.

"How dare you make fun of me!" cried Kate.

Lizzie shook her head fast. "But it wasn't me! I swear. I have no clue—"

"You're *clueless*, all right," snapped Kate. "But I already knew that!"

"Wait, I can explain!" Lizzie said. But she knew she couldn't.

Kate looked at Lizzie as if she were an especially disgusting bug. "News flash, McGuire. You've got yourself a one-way ticket to Loserville. *Forever!*"

Kate and the rest of the cheerleaders turned and marched inside the school.

"Wait!" Lizzie said. "Kate, I need to talk to you!"

"Forget it," Kate told Lizzie over her shoulder. She kept on walking.

"I'm sorry," Lizzie called after her in a small voice. But Kate couldn't hear her by now, anyway. And all the other kids in the quad were staring at her.

O-kay, thought Lizzie. Can things get any worse?

No. And do you know how to spell my social life from this moment on? Gimme an O. Gimme a V. Gimme an E. Gimme an R. (i totally could have been a cheerleader.)

Lizzie sighed. "This never happens to Nancy Drew," she said to Miranda and Gordo. "No one ever thinks *she* committed the crime."

"Actually, people tried to frame Nancy all the time," Carole spoke up. "In the later books, anyway."

"Oh, right," Lizzie said. She'd almost forgotten that Carole was even there.

"You know, no one would be stupid enough to

put her own name in a message like that," Gordo said. "I'm sure Kate realizes that."

"Mmm-hmm," Lizzie replied. But she wasn't really listening. She'd spotted something very peculiar.

Ms. Young was watching them again. From behind a *tree*. The assistant guidance counselor seemed really nervous. And Lizzie could have sworn Ms. Young was talking to herself as she sipped a cup of coffee.

It was almost . . . creepy.

"Guys, look over there," Lizzie said in a low voice. "Do you think Ms. Young is following us?"

"Lizzie, what are you talking about?" Gordo asked.

"Ms. Young. She's moving from tree to tree, like she's *spying* on us."

"Are you sure, Lizzie?" Carole looked around. "Why would a teacher do something like that?"

"What a creepy thought," Miranda said, shuddering.

"I'm telling you, Lizzie, you're totally paranoid," Gordo said. "The stress must be getting to you. Ms. Young isn't even there."

"Huh?" Lizzie frowned and peered toward the trees again.

Gordo was right. Ms. Young had totally vanished!

But Lizzie knew she hadn't *imagined* that the assistant guidance counselor had been there. Ms. Young had left her Styrofoam coffee cup on one of the picnic benches. It was still steaming.

"I am not crazy," Lizzie insisted. "I know what'll happen next. Notes will keep appearing. Kids will start disappearing. And it will all be blamed on *me.*"

Meanwhile, the real villain, who wears a scary mask and has long claws and trails green slime, will continue to spread evil!

"Lizzie, listen to yourself," Gordo said. "That is ridiculous."

"You know, Gordo," Miranda said. "You may change your mind when *you* get one of those mean notes."

"Well, that's never going to happen," Gordo said smugly. "Because I am superobservant and way too smart to be fooled like that."

Lizzie and Miranda just glared at him as they all entered the school building. But Carole looked impressed. She gave Gordo a little flirty smile.

Gordo smiled back.

Suddenly, Carole seemed flustered. "I, um, need to talk to Ms. George about something," she said. She hurried toward the English classroom.

"I think that chick has a crush on me," Gordo said. He sounded pleased.

Lizzie and Miranda rolled their eyes.

"Now, who's making too big a deal about things?" Miranda asked him.

Lizzie had already spotted it, of course. But she said nothing.

"Wait and see," Gordo said.

When the three of them arrived in class a few minutes later, they were greeted at the door by a worried-looking Ethan Craft.

"Ethan, what's wrong?" Lizzie asked anxiously.

Ethan shook his head. "Lizzie, Lizzie, Lizzie," he said. "I thought we were friends. How could you *do* this to me?"

CHAPTER

7

Lizzie's already bad mood took a major nosedive.

Tall, handsome Ethan looked as seriously cool as ever, standing in front of her with his big brown eyes and his longish dirty-blond hair. He wore a black sweater and a pair of worn blue jeans. But it wasn't how he *looked* that upset Lizzie. It was what he *held* in front of him: a tiny paper airplane. A yellow paper airplane with purple writing on one of the wings.

Ugh. Not *another* message.

Lizzie leaned closer and read the purple writing on the wing—

LIZZIE AIR MAIL

"Oh, no," Lizzie murmured.

What *now*? she thought. And why does it have to be *Ethan*?

"Okay, Lizzie," Ethan said. He held up his hands. "You got me. I'll go out with you tonight."

Lizzie's mouth dropped open. So did Miranda's.

You mean you like me? You really, really like me?!

"As, like, a *friend*. Cool?" Ethan said. Then he glanced back inside the classroom. A pretty girl with long, dark hair and a short white dress waved. He waved back, and then he turned to Lizzie and added, "Even if I do have to cancel my hot date with Monique Lafaver."

WHAT?! Lizzie stood frozen in the doorway. Her face burned in total humiliation. And total confusion.

Gordo gave her a nudge. "Lizzie," he whispered. "*Say* something."

Lizzie tried to talk. But no words came out.

Miranda reached over and grabbed the airplane from Ethan. She unfolded it quickly and read the note out loud while Lizzie read it silently over her shoulder.

TONIGHT AT THE DIGITAL BEAN— OR YOUR BIG SECRET WILL BE REVEALED!

Lizzie rubbed her forehead. Whoever wrote

this note wanted her to meet Ethan at the Digital Bean—the cybercafé where the Hillridge kids hung out. But why? Lizzie wondered.

"Whoa," Gordo said. "Your big secret will be revealed, huh? What secret is that?"

Ethan frowned. "For me to know, *Gor-don*. And you *not* to find out."

Lizzie felt terrible. "Ethan, I didn't—" she began to explain.

But just then, Ms. George came to the door. "Chop, chop, people. The world of mystery waits for no one."

"Catch you tonight, Lizzie," Ethan said. Then he disappeared inside the classroom.

"Way to go, Lizzie!" Miranda squealed.

"I don't even know how to make an airplane out of a sticky note!" Lizzie wailed.

"Who cares?" Miranda pushed Lizzie into class. "It worked, didn't it? You have a date with Ethan!"

"Yeah." Lizzie sighed. "Sort of."

Ms. George called the class to order. "So, everyone," she said, "how are our mystery stories going so far?"

Lizzie saw Carole smile at Gordo from across the room. "She definitely likes me," Gordo whispered to Lizzie.

For the rest of class, Lizzie and Miranda passed notes. To each other. Normal ones, in pencil on lined white paper.

"Just meet him at the Bean as planned," Miranda wrote. "Sometime during the date you can tell him you didn't send that weird message. Why blow a major opportunity?"

Miranda does have a point there, Lizzie told herself.

Besides, she was thrilled about the idea of a date with Ethan. And as a bonus, she was even going to find out some big secret he had.

Hmmm, Lizzie thought. What could *that* be? Maybe he has a secret crush on someone. Like me!

Hey, come on. What would Nancy Drew do in this situation? Not that she ever had any problem getting Ned Nickerson to notice her.

Lizzie drummed her nails on her desk. *If the mysterious note writer wants me and Ethan to get together at the Bean,* thought Lizzie, *then I'll bet the note writer will probably be there, too. Watching.*

And that *means . . .*

"We need to do a stakeout," Lizzie scribbled back to Miranda. "Can you help?"

"Elementary, my dear Lizzie," Miranda replied. "Gordo and I will be there!"

When the bell rang, everyone rushed for the door. Lizzie walked out with Miranda and Gordo. "I can't believe I have a date with Ethan tonight," she said dreamily.

"A fake one," Gordo pointed out. Miranda gave him a warning jab with her elbow.

"Listen, Gordo, I *have* to go to the Bean tonight," Lizzie said. "Because we need to set a trap for the note writer."

"You mean Kate," Miranda said.

"Maybe," Lizzie said. "Or . . . maybe not. But this will be the perfect way to reveal the person's identity. Once and for all."

Lizzie began to tell Gordo and Miranda her plan. Well, it wasn't a plan, exactly. Not yet. She was kind of making things up as she went along. Sometimes detectives had to do that.

And sometimes they left their casebook in English class. *Oops.*

"I've got to go back," Lizzie told her friends. "You guys go on without me, okay? I'll be right there."

Lizzie ran back down the hall. Her notebook was right where she'd left it, on her desk. Lizzie grabbed it and hurried to her next class. On the way, she passed Ms. Young's office door.

Lizzie glanced inside. She couldn't help being curious. The assistant guidance counselor was just so . . . strange. What exactly did she do all day? Hardly any kids at Hillridge ever went to see her.

Ms. Young was drinking a cup of coffee and speaking into a little tape recorder. Lizzie hid behind the door and tried to listen.

"Teen Subject Number Twenty-three," Lizzie heard her say. "Social skills in decline. Clearly folding under pressure."

Lizzie frowned. *Whoa!* She thought. *Waitie* just a sec!

Ms. Young had been sneaking around, following them. Had she actually been taking *notes* on Lizzie and her friends?

Lizzie shuddered. That was so . . . creepy.

Could she, Lizzie McGuire, be Teen Subject Number Twenty-three?

CHAPTER

8

Lizzie tiptoed away from Ms. Young's door. Note to self, she thought—add assistant guidance counselor to Official Suspect List.

She headed quickly for the gym. Now that she thought about it, Ms. Young had been acting even more suspiciously than Kate.

Hadn't Ms. Young been snooping around everywhere?

Maybe she wasn't just *taking* notes. Maybe she was *writing* them!

But that doesn't make sense, Lizzie thought. Ms. Young had no motive. What kind of bizarre-o reason could a teacher have to upset a bunch of kids?

And why would she pick on *me*? Lizzie asked herself. Ms. Young was new at Hillridge. So, there was no "history" between them or anything like that.

On the other hand, Kate *did* have a motive.

Lizzie sighed. Once upon a time, Kate had been really *happy* that Lizzie had found Mr. Stewart Wugglesby. Back before Kate had made the cheerleading squad and turned into a ferocious, snobby she-beast.

Just then, Lizzie spotted Hannah Marvin. She was getting her gym uniform out of her locker.

"Hannah!" Lizzie said, hurrying up to her.

Hannah looked startled. But at least she didn't run in terror. "Hey, Lizzie," she said, biting her lip. "I really need to talk to you."

"No, *I* need to talk to *you*," Lizzie said. "About

that note you got. The one that said, 'I know what you did last week—'"

"Lizzie, I *so* didn't mean to do it," Hannah broke in. "I mean, last week, I did kiss Larry Tudgeman at Lauren Silverman's party. He told me you kissed him one time, too. But I had no idea you still liked him, I swear. You don't have to threaten me. Larry's all yours!"

No way! Me? Kiss Tudgeman? Frog prince of all geeks? Talk about warts!

"Ohmigosh, Hannah, I don't *like* Larry!" Lizzie said. "I mean, not that way. I mean, *really*, he's all yours! And I never *kissed* him—it was just stupid health class CPR lessons! And I didn't send you that note to warn you off Larry, either. I didn't send you that note at all. It was obviously somebody's idea of a joke."

Hannah sighed. "Well, I don't know who sent it, but I'm glad you didn't. I mean, I don't like to think I'm wrong about people. And I always thought you were a nice person."

At least *someone* at Hillridge still thinks so, Lizzie told herself.

Hannah shut her locker door. "Sorry, I have to go. I'm late for gym. See ya." She waved and hurried down the hall.

Lizzie leaned back against the wall and took a deep breath. She was late for gym, too. And she hadn't solved the case yet. But at least things were beginning to look up.

Suddenly, Larry Tudgeman came loping down the hall. "I got one!" he shouted to anyone who cared to listen. "I got a note from Lizzie McGuire! She's in love with me!"

Cringing, Lizzie ducked behind a broken locker door, banging her head as Larry rushed past. No way was she going to ask to see *that* bogus message.

That is one clue i do *not* need.

After school, as Lizzie walked toward her house, she saw something move. It was the lilac bush below the McGuires' kitchen window.

Yikes, Lizzie thought. That is *not* the wind. Someone is *in* that bush. Could it be an intruder? Or even—the note writer?

She walked toward the bush very quietly. Then she peered down.

Okay, come on out with your hands UP! You have the right to remain silent!

Lizzie spotted two pairs of dirty basketball sneakers. And four jeans-covered legs.

"Hey!" she shouted.

The bush rustled loudly. Then two heads poked out between the branches. One was dark and curly. The other was wearing a Sherlock Holmes–style deerstalker hat with a *Detective Dude* logo.

"What are you two *doing*?" Lizzie asked.

Matt crawled out of the lilac bush. "Shhhh," he said. "You're being recorded."

"Excuse me?" Lizzie said.

Her little brother stood up and brushed off his cheap vinyl trench coat. Then he patted his fake mustache. "Lanny and I are monitoring Mom," he explained. "Using my handy-dandy, new *Detective Dude* Super Surveillance Camera." He held up a small, plastic gizmo.

Lizzie looked through the kitchen window. As Mrs. McGuire fixed dinner, she was dancing around with a pot holder. And *singing*.

"Give me that!" Lizzie said. She reached out for Matt's camera and pulled out the tape. "You can't spy on Mom. Or any other family members."

"Hey, you're just jealous," Matt said. "Because *you're* a lousy detective."

Lanny nodded and crossed his arms.

Lizzie gave up. She left the two of them to their little-boy games and went into the house.

"Hi, Mom!" she called as she ran upstairs. She dropped her knapsack on her bed and headed to the bathroom to check her hair.

Lizzie sighed when she looked in the bathroom mirror. Her hair was a tangled mess. She definitely needed to wash and curl it before her big date, er . . . *stakeout*, she corrected herself.

That reminded Lizzie that she should make a few notes in her casebook.

Unpleasant as the idea might be, she probably needed to question Larry Tudgeman about the fake love note.

She shuddered at the very idea. Then she walked from the bathroom back to her bedroom and took her casebook out of her knapsack.

As she looked through it, she saw a yellow note stuck on one of the pages.

Nooo! Lizzie told herself. Not possible. At all.

"At least there's no purple writing on it this time," Lizzie muttered aloud.

Then she looked at the page itself. Obviously, she had spoken too soon.

Scrawled across the page, just under her latest English notes, was a new message in smeared purple ink:

SURRENDER, McGUIRE!
YOU'RE TOO LATE
TO SOLVE THIS CASE!

Lizzie screamed and dropped her notebook.

How had the note writer gotten into her *bedroom*?

She was totally freaked out now.

Lizzie looked under the bed. She checked under her desk, too. Then she threw open the closet door.

No one was there. *Phew!* She dropped onto her bed in relief.

Then she bounced straight back up. Only one short, evil person could have sneaked into her room while she'd been checking her hair in the bathroom.

"MATT!" Lizzie cried at the top of her lungs.

She tore out of her room and down the stairs. But as she reached the bottom step, she came to a halt.

Her mom was standing in the living room, shaking a finger at Matt and Lanny.

"Don't let me *ever* catch you two spying on me again," she scolded.

HA! Busted! *Now* who's a lousy detective?

"Matt's been spying on me, too," Lizzie said, walking up to the three of them. "He just went through my knapsack about five minutes ago."

Mrs. McGuire sighed and rubbed her brow. She looked very tired. "No, honey," she said.

"I've been interrogating your brother and his chatterbox buddy here ever since you got home. Matt could not possibly have been in your bedroom. Not this time, anyway."

Matt threw her one of his sickeningly sweet smiles. "You lose, rat-breath," he silently mouthed.

Lizzie squinted at him. "Guess you're off the hook, twerp," she told him. "For now." She turned and stomped back upstairs.

Lizzie had to admit, her annoying little bro couldn't have been responsible for the other creepy notes, either. Matt wouldn't be able to step a sneaker toe into Hillridge without a serious disguise. And a major instant growth spurt. Principal Tweedy remembered Matt McGuire— very vividly—from his short-lived pose as one of Lizzie's classmates.

Lizzie ignored the notebook on her bedroom floor. Right now, she had to concentrate on getting ready for tonight.

i have to look especially gorgeous for the big date out. Um, i mean, *stakeout*. Anything for Ethan. Er, i mean, *the case*.

Even though the Digital Bean was close to the McGuires' house, Lizzie's mom insisted on driving her since it was pouring rain.

Why did I bother curling my hair? Lizzie wondered.

In this humidity, she was fated to look like a frizzy-haired mess, no matter how many hair-care products she used.

Let's recap: Ethan *finally* makes a date to meet me after school, and i get the worst bad-hair day of my life. Can you say, "Life reeks"?

"Remember, call me if you want a ride back!" Mrs. McGuire shouted as Lizzie made a break for it. "The storm's supposed to last all night."

Lizzie nodded and ducked through the door of the Bean. The place was packed with Hillridge kids. With luck, none of them had seen her mom.

She finally spotted Miranda and Gordo. Both of them pretended not to notice her. That was part of The Plan. Miranda jerked her head toward the booth right behind them.

Ethan was pouring a whole shaker of sugar into his latte. He looked totally nervous.

"Hi, Ethan," Lizzie said brightly. She slid into the vinyl seat across from him.

Lizzie had dressed with extra care, of course. She'd worn her jeans skirt, cool faux lizard boots, and her long-sleeved pink sparkle top. A matching band sparkled in her slightly frizzy blond hair.

"Oh, uh, hi, Lizzie." Ethan smiled weakly at her, then glanced longingly across the room at

Monique Lafaver. She was sitting with some guys from the swim team—and Kate.

Aha! Lizzie thought, ignoring Ethan's pathetic obsession with Monique. Something more important had caught Lizzie's attention: Suspect Number One was in the house!

But so was half the school. And Lizzie was sure they were all staring at her.

Because I'm on a date with Ethan? Lizzie wondered. Or because everyone thinks I'm a horrible person, thanks to those nasty notes?

"So, anyway, it was all my stepmom's idea," Ethan was saying. "Actually, she kind of tricked me into it. Then it was, like, out of control."

Lizzie snapped back to attention.

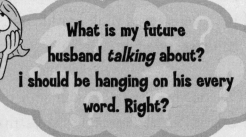

What is my future husband *talking* about? i should be hanging on his every word. Right?

Ethan looked puzzled. "Uh, Lizzie, did you hear what I just said? I thought you wanted to talk to me about the big secret and all."

Lizzie nodded. "Oh, yeah. I did, didn't I? I mean, sort of. I don't have to, or anything."

"I just didn't know I had to do the whole vitamin thing," Ethan went on. "I mean, all that cutesy baby stuff is just not my scene. And I don't even *take* vitamins."

From the corner of her eye, Lizzie saw Carole come into the Bean. That's funny, she thought. Carole never goes anywhere.

Then she noticed Carole glancing at Gordo. When Gordo waved, she blushed.

Bingo, Lizzie thought. Maybe Carole really *did* like him!

"So that's the deal," Ethan finished. "That's my big secret."

"Oh," said Lizzie. "Oh?"

Lizzie stared blankly at Ethan.

What is? she wondered.

How rude is it to ask your crush-boy to please repeat the entire story he just told you because you weren't paying attention?

Ethan leaned across the table. "Listen, Lizzie, I'd really appreciate it if you would keep all this quiet. Okay?"

Lizzie frantically wracked her brain. *What* in the world had Ethan been babbling on about? Something about his stepmom . . . and cutesy baby stuff . . . and vitamins . . . ?

Hello, may I please speak to me? FOCUS!

I can't believe this, Lizzie thought. Ethan Craft just spilled his guts to me. And I have *no clue* what he said.

Suddenly, a crash of thunder shook the room. Silverware and coffee cups rattled.

Lizzie turned to see a bolt of lightning streak past the window—and Ms. Young walk into the Digital Bean.

The assistant guidance counselor was sopping wet. She headed straight to the coffee counter.

Lizzie was instantly suspicious. Why is Ms. Young coming to the school hangout for her coffee? she wondered. Didn't she, like, want a break from seeing students all day? Maybe the woman was up to something.

But Lizzie *still* couldn't figure out why Ms. Young would send creepy notes to a bunch of students. That would be totally weird. And she'd lose her job for sure.

Hmmm, Lizzie thought. Her *job* might be the answer. Ms. Young's office was always empty.

Maybe she felt unneeded. Maybe she was trying to upset everyone so she had a *reason* to help them.

"Hi, Ethan." Kate slid into the booth beside him. Then she looked at Lizzie. "Oh, hi, Loo-zie. What are *you* doing here? Don't you have a seven-thirty curfew?"

"Seven-thirty? That's harsh," Ethan said. Then he turned to Kate. "Hey, Kate, you didn't hear what we were talking about, did you?"

"No," Kate said. "But I'm a very good listener." She squinted at Lizzie.

Lizzie sighed. This "date" wasn't turning out so well. But at least both of her suspects had shown up. *Hmmm*, she thought. Why *did* Kate sit down with me and Ethan?

Just then, there was another crash of thunder. And everyone screamed—because the Digital Bean had just gone dark.

10

O-kay.

Lizzie was now sitting in a dark coffeehouse with a bunch of screaming Hillridge kids. And it was definitely not fun—especially since she wasn't the one snuggled up right next to Ethan Craft.

Kate was.

"Can't somebody *do* something?" called the cheer queen.

Less than a minute later, the coffeehouse lights came back on.

"That's better," Kate said.

Lizzie sighed. Even the electricity did whatever Kate wanted.

Gordo came up to their table. "Lizzie, I need to talk to you," he said.

Lizzie raised an eyebrow. This wasn't part of The Plan.

"Right now," Gordo said. "It's important."

"Okay, okay." Lizzie slid out of the booth. She followed Gordo to the back of the room, near the coffee counter.

"Look what I just got," Gordo said. "I can't believe it."

He held out a yellow sticky note.

"Excellent!" Lizzie said. She grabbed the note eagerly.

"Someone put it on the back of my shirt in the dark," Gordo said.

"Are you sure?" Lizzie asked.

Gordo looked annoyed. "Yes, I'm sure. It's not like my mom slapped it on me as I was going out the door tonight!"

Lizzie read the message:

PRIDE GOES BEFORE A FALL. WATCH YOUR STEP.

"Same purple handwriting," she said. "It looks like mine, but it isn't. And it's signed 'Your Friend.' But you know it wasn't me, right?"

"Duh," said Gordo. "Of course, I know that! But what do you think the message *means*?"

"I have no idea," Lizzie said. "So, okay. Who was near your table when the lights went out?"

Gordo didn't seem to hear her. "I can't believe someone actually got past me like that."

"Gordo," Lizzie said. "I'm working on a case here. Do you remember anyone coming up to you? Was anyone near you and Miranda at all?"

"I don't know," Gordo said. "It was dark."

Lizzie sighed. Gordo wasn't as helpful as Nancy Drew's friends. "Well, one thing's for sure," she said. "It wasn't Kate."

"Miranda and I were sitting right behind you guys," Gordo pointed out.

"True," Lizzie said. "But Kate was on the other side of the booth. And as far as I know, she was right there beside Ethan the entire time. She was complaining nonstop about the lights being off."

"Maybe one of Kate's friends could have done it," Gordo suggested.

Lizzie shook her head. "Nope. They were all hanging out with a bunch of guys from the swim team. So that leaves . . ."

She turned toward Ms. Young. The assistant guidance counselor was sitting at a table by the door. She seemed to be mumbling to herself again. And *watching* everyone.

Lizzie shivered.

Hold on, she thought. Ms. Young would have had to sprint all the way across the room to Gordo and back again before the lights came on. Still . . .

"I'm going to have to question Ms. Young," Lizzie told Gordo.

"Ms. Young? Why?" Gordo asked.

Lizzie filled him in on what she'd overheard outside the assistant guidance counselor's office.

"I don't know, Lizzie," Gordo said. "That sounds kind of far-fetched to me. I mean, come on. Subject Twenty-three? You've been reading too many detective stories."

"Well, that's what I heard," Lizzie insisted. "And a good detective has good ears."

Not hearing Ethan's secret doesn't count. Besides, from now on, i'm totally gonna be all business!

The whole time Lizzie was talking to Gordo, she was closely watching Ms. Young. But suddenly, the assistant guidance counselor looked straight at Lizzie and frowned.

"Ohmigosh!" Lizzie whispered. "She knows I'm watching her."

"Let's go back to the booth," Gordo said. "Miranda must be wondering what's up." He waved to their friend across the room. "And don't worry about your date being left hanging. Looks to me like Kate's keeping him company."

Lizzie sighed. Sure enough, Ethan and Kate looked pretty cozy. Well, to be honest, Kate was the one who looked cozy. Ethan looked seriously miserable. Monique Lafaver was having a grand old time over at the swim team table—and Ethan couldn't take his eyes off her.

Speaking of eyes, thought Lizzie, as she followed Gordo to the booth—Ms. Young, Suspect Number Two, was still watching her.

But when she and Ms. Young locked gazes this time, a funny expression came over the assistant guidance counselor's face.

"She looks . . . totally guilty," Lizzie whispered to Gordo. "And really, really nervous."

Ms. Young began to gather her things.

"Oh, no!" Lizzie said. "She's going to leave! We have to follow her!"

By now, she and Gordo had reached the booth where Miranda was sitting. "Miranda, let's go!" Lizzie said urgently. Then she leaned over to the next booth, the one where Ethan and Kate were sitting. "Ethan, I'm really, really sorry," she said. "But something's come up. I've got to go. Why don't you go over and talk to Monique?"

"Uh, sure, Lizzie," Ethan said. "Whatever."

"Monique?" Kate said.

"And don't worry, your secret's safe with me," Lizzie added.

"Secret?" Kate said.

Oops. But Lizzie didn't have time to waste. She looked back at Ms. Young again.

The assistant guidance counselor seemed even more nervous now. She jumped up and hurried out of the Bean, knocking over her nearly empty coffee cup.

"Come on!" Lizzie said to Miranda and Gordo. "Follow that suspect!"

The three of them ran out into the rain.

"Will someone please clue me in here?" Miranda asked. "What are we *doing*?"

But Lizzie didn't have time to answer. Across the street, Suspect Number Two was hopping into her getaway car.

Lizzie ran up, just as Ms. Young had finished locking the door. She didn't seem to notice Lizzie.

Or she's *pretending* not to notice, Lizzie thought.

Through the foggy, rain-streaked window, she saw a thick textbook on the passenger seat. The title said *Psychology* in big letters. And there was a yellow bookmark sticking out from the pages!

Aha! Lizzie told herself. A yellow sticky note! There was probably a whole pack of them in the car somewhere.

"Ms. Young!" Lizzie called through the pouring rain.

But the suspect had already gunned the engine. The car peeled away down the street.

Lizzie just stood in the rain, watching the taillights disappear. "I can't believe she got away," she said.

"Believe it," Miranda said behind her. Her teeth were chattering. "Can we go back inside now?"

Lizzie turned around. Miranda and Gordo were totally soaked. And so was she.

"Sorry, guys," Lizzie said. "I guess I got a little carried away."

"No problem," Gordo said. "We understand. You're on a case."

Miranda nodded. "R-r-right," she said. "Can we call your mom to give us a ride?"

"Sure," Lizzie said. Then she held out her arms and twirled in the rain. "I've finally found my culprit!" she cried. "*Yeeessss!* Mystery solved!"

Move over, Sherlock Holmes!
You're not all that!

On the way home, Lizzie decided she was going to talk to Ms. Young at school the first thing tomorrow. And with luck, her own rep at Hillridge would be restored by lunchtime!

Good-bye, "Lizzie the Loser." Hello, "McGuire for Hire," Hillridge's very own supersleuth!

CHAPTER

11

Lizzie arrived at school bright and early the next morning. She marched straight to Ms. Young's office.

It was time to question the "alleged perp." That meant the person who might have done a crime. The cops on her dad's favorite TV show said it all the time.

Lizzie thought "alleged perp" sounded pretty cool. Even better than "suspect."

Suspect was *so* last century, she thought.

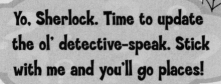

Yo, Sherlock. Time to update the ol' detective-speak. Stick with me and you'll go places!

Unfortunately, the assistant guidance counselor wasn't there. Lizzie waited outside, tapping her foot.

Where the heck *is* she? Lizzie thought. Could there be some kind of guidance emergency or something?

The hallway was still empty. Classes wouldn't start for a few more minutes. Lizzie frowned. Was Ms. Young not going to show up?

She peered around the office door. It looked as if Ms. Young had been there. And not very long ago, either. There was a cup of still-steaming coffee on her desk. As usual.

Ms. Young sure does drink a lot of coffee, Lizzie thought.

Then she saw what was next to the coffee

cup—the psychology textbook Lizzie had seen in Ms. Young's car the night before!

Lizzie looked both ways to see whether anyone was coming. Then she ducked into the assistant guidance counselor's office.

It's okay for me to be in here, Lizzie told herself. I'm only going to take a quick peek. It's all in the name of justice—or something like that.

Ms. Young's office was very cluttered. There were books and papers everywhere.

The yellow bookmark was still sticking out of the psychology book. "Excellent!" Lizzie said aloud. She eagerly picked up the book.

Just then, the first bell rang. Lizzie froze in panic as kids began crowding into the hall. Someone was going to see her!

Almost without thinking, Lizzie stuffed the heavy book into her knapsack. I'm just going to borrow it, she told herself. I *have* to. It's *evidence*.

She backed out into the hall just as Miranda and Gordo were coming by.

"Whew! I'm so glad you guys are here," Lizzie told them.

"So, how did it go?" Miranda asked. "What did Ms. Young say?"

"Did she confess to the crime?" Gordo asked.

Lizzie shook her head. "I never even got a chance to question her. But check this out." She showed her friends the book inside her knapsack.

"Maybe Ms. Young has been using it to look up a cure for her weirdness," Lizzie said.

"Possible," Gordo said. "But highly unlikely. I did a bit of research last night in my parents' library."

"Really?" Lizzie asked. "Gee, thanks. That's great." Gordo's parents were both psychiatrists. "What did you find out?"

"Well, Ms. Young's personality is extremely interesting," Gordo said. "But she doesn't seem to fit any of the profiles I read about."

"Like what?" Miranda was getting impatient.

"Like paranoia," Gordo said. "You know,

when a person thinks everyone is out to get them. On the other hand, Lizzie here fits that profile very nicely—"

"Hey!" Lizzie began to protest. But her words were drowned out by Principal Tweedy's voice over the school's public address system.

"LIZZIE McGUIRE, REPORT TO MY OFFICE IMMEDIATELY! LIZZIE McGUIRE."

"Me?" Lizzie squeaked. "Why does Principal Tweedy want to talk to *me*?"

"Nice knowing you, Lizzie," Miranda said, putting her hand on Lizzie's shoulder. "You've been a good friend."

"Don't worry, Lizzie," Gordo said. "No big deal. Maybe you forgot your lunch or something, and your mom brought it."

"I'm buying my lunch today," Lizzie said.

"Well, you'd better get moving," Miranda said. "You know how Principal Tweedy feels about lateness."

Lizzie sighed. "See you in class. I hope."

She hurried toward the main office. When she got there, a bunch of kids were already waiting to see Principal Tweedy.

Hey, wait! i didn't do anything wrong! So why do i feel so . . . guilty?

"You here for detention assignments?" one of them asked her. "Get in line."

Lizzie went to the end of the line and put down her heavy knapsack. Then she remembered. The knapsack! Inside it she had Ms. Young's psychology textbook—with the yellow sticky-note evidence!

Ms. Young must have reported the book stolen, Lizzie realized. Maybe she even saw me leave her office and assumed I'd taken it. *Yikes!*

"McGuire?" Principal Tweedy came to the door. "You're next."

Lizzie followed him into his office. It was a lot neater than Ms. Young's.

"I'll get right to the point, Ms. McGuire," the principal said. "I've been out of town this week attending a very important School Administrators of America party." He cleared his throat. "Er, *convention*."

"That's nice," Lizzie said politely.

The principal frowned.

"And I came back to find a stack of student complaints against Lizzie McGuire on my desk," he said. Then he nodded toward a pile of square yellow sticky notes under a large frowny-face paperweight.

Lizzie gulped. This *definitely* never happened to Sherlock Holmes. Or Nancy Drew.

Principal Tweedy crossed his arms. "Do we have an explanation for this?"

Lizzie gulped again.

An explanation?
Of course! Sure, we do! i just have
to think of one. (Gee, i could *really*
use that cat who solves crimes about now.
Or even Matt's stupid *Detective Dude*
bunny gumshoe. Either one
works for me!)

"Well . . . um . . ." Lizzie didn't know what to say. Honesty is the best policy, she reminded herself. She told Principal Tweedy all about the notes. And Ms. Young.

When she had finished, Principal Tweedy looked confused. And very doubtful.

He stood up from his desk. "All right, Ms. McGuire. We're going down to Ms. Young's office," he said. "Right now."

Lizzie nodded. Good, she thought. Now everything would be cleared up.

She hoped.

Principal Tweedy knocked on Ms. Young's door. The assistant guidance counselor looked up. As soon as she saw them, her hands started to shake.

See? Lizzie wanted to say. Look how nervous she is. She's totally guilty!

"Wait here," the principal told Lizzie.

Principal Tweedy stayed in Ms. Young's office a long time. When he came out, his face was grim. He took Lizzie by the elbow and walked her back down the hall.

"It seems Ms. Young is taking a night course in teen psychology at the university," he said. "She wants to be promoted to full guidance counselor here at Hillridge."

But she's the crazy note writer! Lizzie wanted to shout. Instead she said, "R-really? How interesting."

"Yes," Principal Tweedy said. "She's doing research on teen peer pressure. That's why she has been observing you students. She takes notes by speaking into a small tape recorder."

So, Ms. Young wasn't really muttering to herself, Lizzie thought. *Oops!* The assistant guidance counselor's explanation actually sounded acceptable.

Except for one thing.

"Wait!" Lizzie said. She stopped in the hall and pulled Ms. Young's big psychology textbook out of her knapsack. "I forgot to show you *this*, Principal Tweedy. Here's my evidence against Ms. Young." She snatched the yellow paper from between the pages and held it out.

But it wasn't a creepy message. Or even a square yellow sticky note.

It was a night parking pass from the university! The alleged perp was telling the truth!

Oh, no!

The only thing Ms. Young was guilty of was drinking too much coffee, Lizzie realized. It was the caffeine that must have made her superjittery. Not guilt!

"I'll continue to look into the matter of those student complaints, Ms. McGuire," Principal Tweedy said. "In the meantime, please return Ms. Young's property and pick up your detention assignments from my office on Monday. You'll be needing them for the next two weeks."

When the principal had gone, Lizzie slumped against the wall. She didn't know what was worse: getting two weeks of undeserved detention or failing to solve this case.

Lizzie sat in English class, feeling totally miserable.

The whole school was talking about the mysterious note writer—Lizzie McGuire.

She just knew it.

Who knows how many notes are out there by now? she thought. There are probably zillions I don't even know about. Yet.

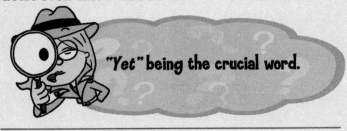

"*Yet*" being the crucial word.

Lizzie doodled in her notebook as Ms. George droned on about famous modern mystery writers.

Maybe I should write to the Nancy Drew author, Carolyn Keene, Lizzie told herself. I need to ask her a few questions. Like, how can I get myself out of this one?

Was it harder to write *fake* mysteries? Or solve *real* ones?

Lizzie had no clue. But right now, the Case of the Nasty Notes seemed impossible to crack.

She flipped back through her English notebook. On the first day of class with Ms. George, her notes had been a lot cooler looking.

I really loved that purple pen, Lizzie thought.

But now she didn't care if she never saw anything purple again.

"So, now we have our pieces of the detective puzzle," Ms. George said. She wrote on the blackboard. "Crime, clues, suspects, motives. And what is the next step to unlocking a mystery? Anyone?"

**i know! i know!
How about dumb luck?**

Carole immediately raised her hand. Lizzie noticed she was wearing purple nail polish today. Very un-Carole.

The girl was constantly chewing her fingernails. So that polish wouldn't last very long, anyway.

She's probably just trying to impress Gordo, Lizzie thought.

"Observation," Carole answered. "And the next step is deduction."

The teacher beamed. "Excellent, Carole!" she said. "You certainly have learned a lot from your mom."

Carole blushed. "Thanks, Ms. George."

"Show-off," Lizzie muttered under her breath.

She couldn't help it. Carole thought she knew everything about solving mysteries.

Ha! Lizzie thought. I'd like to see her try to solve *this* one.

She considered asking Carole for help. For about a nanosecond.

No way, Lizzie told herself. I'm going to find the mysterious note writer myself. No matter what it takes!

She squeezed her eyes shut. Step by step, she worked her way back through the case.

Where had she gone wrong? What clue had she missed?

Suddenly, Lizzie sat up straight. "I've got it!" she cried.

Everyone in the class turned to stare at her.

"Lizzie?" Ms. George asked. "You have the answer?"

"The notebook," Lizzie said.

Yikes! Lizzie thought. Did I actually say that? *Out loud?*

But Ms. George just nodded. "Very good, Lizzie. The casebook is indeed one of a detective's most important tools. What are some others? People?"

Lizzie sighed in relief. A narrow escape from total humiliation—possibly a first. But I'm right about the notebook, she told herself. In more ways than one.

The night before, Lizzie had accused Matt of writing in it. But he hadn't. Which meant someone at school had done it.

Lizzie tried to think through her movements in school the day before.

I had my notebook with me most of the day, she told herself. And it was out of my possession only once, for a couple of minutes.

Lizzie flipped back a few pages to double-check where her notes from the day before had left off.

Bingo!

Right at the end of yesterday's English class notes were these words:

SURRENDER, McGUIRE!
YOU'RE TOO LATE
TO SOLVE THIS CASE!

That could only mean one thing. The mysterious note writer was in her English class!

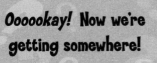

Oooookay! **Now we're getting somewhere!**

The note writer was in her English class and *also* had to have been at the Digital Bean last night.

She glanced around. Just about everyone here had been at the Digital Bean last night!

This wasn't going to be easy, thought Lizzie.

She puzzled over it some more.

The note writer had to have had a *motive* as

well as opportunity. So, who did that sound like?

Lizzie began to glance around the room. Could it have been—

Miranda, no.

Gordo, no.

Ethan, no.

Kate, *probably* no. But still possible.

Hannah, no.

Claire, no.

Tudgeman, no.

She shuddered. With luck, she'd never have to ask him about that bogus Lizzie-loves-you note. She was putting that off—for as long as possible!

Ms. George asked the class another question. Carole's purple fingernails shot up into the air again.

Does that girl *ever* give it a rest? Lizzie thought. Carole was really starting to bug her. Was she up for Mystery Expert of the Year?

Wait a second, Lizzie thought, frowning. What was the deal with Carole's purple nails?

They looked . . . really fake. Press-ons, probably. Or . . .

She leaned forward in her seat to get a better look. Yep, press-ons. But it wasn't just Carole's nails that were purple. Her fingers were kind of purple, too.

As if her pen had exploded. A pen with *purple ink.*

Lizzie drummed her own nails on the desk.

Hmmm . . . she thought. Here's some deduction for you, Carole.

She quickly began to scribble these notes in her casebook.

One: You are in my English class.

Two: You were in the cafeteria when I got the first note.

Three: You could have taken my purple pen because I had it with me. And you've got purple ink all over your fingers.

Four: You were already at school the morning Kate and the cheerleaders got the teddy notes.

Five: You could have put the note on Gordo's shirt at the Digital Bean.

"Call it a hunch, Carole," Lizzie muttered. "From one detective to another, I'd say you're about to get busted!"

13

Lizzie grabbed Miranda and Gordo on the way out of English class. "I need your help," she said.

"At your service," Gordo said. "As always."

Lizzie waited until all the other kids had left. Especially Carole.

"Bye, Gordo," Carole said. She waved her purple fingers at him as she passed.

"Bye," Gordo said. His eyebrows rose, and a stupid smile spread across his face like he was all happy with himself just because some girl was crushin' on him.

Guys. Why are they so easily distracted? Gordo's as bad as Ethan!

"Can we please focus on something important here?" Lizzie asked.

"Sure, Lizzie," Miranda said. "What's up?"

"I've had a breakthrough on the case," Lizzie said. She filled her friends in on what she had figured out in class.

"So, the mystery note writer is *Carole*?" Miranda announced loudly.

"Shh!" Lizzie said, looking around.

"No. No way," said Gordo. "That can't be right. She's so . . ."

"So what?" snapped Lizzie.

Gordo shrugged. "Harmless."

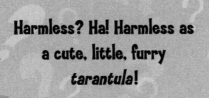

Harmless? Ha! Harmless as a cute, little, furry tarantula!

"Just trust me. She's guilty, okay?" said Lizzie. "And I need you guys to help me toss her stuff."

"Toss it?" Miranda asked. "Toss it where?"

Lizzie sighed. "Toss means to *search* in detective-speak. I want to go through all of Carole's things. Her locker. Her knapsack."

Miranda's eyes widened. "Really?"

"Um, Lizzie, how many weeks of detention did you say Principal Tweedy just gave you?" Gordo asked. "Are you going for the record?"

"No," Lizzie said. "Of course not. We're not actually going to break into Carole's locker. Or steal her knapsack or anything like that. We're just going to sneak a tiny peek."

Gordo and Miranda gave each other worried looks.

"Guys," Lizzie said. "It's just a little snooping. For a very good cause."

Miranda looked doubtful. "And that would be . . . ?"

Lizzie threw up her hands. "To clear my name!" she said. "And stop those nasty notes once and for all."

"Okay," Gordo said. "Count me in. What do you want me to do?" He struck a martial arts pose. "I hope it involves some action. 'Cause that's just the kind of guy I am."

Lizzie smiled. "Don't worry, Gordo. You have a *very* important role in this part of the investigation."

Gordo puffed up his chest.

"You're going to detain the suspect," Lizzie told him sweetly. "Because she has such a big crush on you."

Gordo's face fell. "Oh," he said. "Gee, thanks."

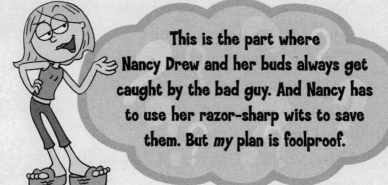

This is the part where Nancy Drew and her buds always get caught by the bad guy. And Nancy has to use her razor-sharp wits to save them. But *my* plan is foolproof.

At twelve-fifty sharp, exactly ten minutes before science class, Gordo took up his position at Carole's locker.

Lizzie and Miranda ducked behind a nearby corner.

"Are you sure she's going to show up?" Miranda asked.

Lizzie nodded. "She has to," she said. "She needs to get her safety goggles for lab."

Sure enough, Carole showed up at twelve-fifty-two. Science was only eight minutes away.

"Carole, hi!" Gordo said. "How's it going?"

"Oh, hi, Gordo," she said brightly.

Gordo just stood there, staring.

"Um, excuse me, I'm sorry," said Carole, "but you're blocking my locker."

"I am?" Gordo jumped away. "Oh, gee, sorry. Here, I'll move down the hall a little."

Lizzie cringed. Don't blow it, Gordo, she told him silently.

But Carole didn't seem suspicious. She twirled the combination on her locker door and opened it.

"Listen, Carole," Gordo said. "I need your help. Like, right now."

"Oh," Carole said. "Okay, I guess, as long as it doesn't take too long. I don't like being late for my classes."

"No problem," Gordo said. "You see, I'm really, really in trouble. With . . . um . . ." He looked quickly back at Lizzie.

She held up her English notebook and waved it at him.

"With my . . . um, mystery story," Gordo said. "And you're the only who can help me. You know everything about solving mysteries."

"That's true," Carole said.

Lizzie could see she was buying it. Gordo had pulled it off.

"So, what's the problem?" Carole asked Gordo.

Gordo walked a little way down the hall, bringing Carole with him. "Well, it's the whole motive thing," he said. "My main character, Sergeant Sylvester Sylvester, is—"

"Now's our chance!" Lizzie whispered to Miranda. "Come on, let's make this quick!"

The two of them dove toward Carole's locker. Miranda searched the top shelf. Lizzie took the main cubby.

Nothing.

Miranda shrugged helplessly.

Lizzie looked down at Carole's knapsack. She'd left it on the floor in front of her locker. Big mistake, Carole. Lizzie pounced on it with glee.

Eureka!

Lizzie found three square pads of yellow sticky notes. And she stuck her hand in a still wet glob of purple ink from her exploded pen.

Yuck. Lizzie quickly wiped her purple-stained fingers on her dark jeans.

Then she gasped.

Carole's English notebook was in her knapsack. And the front of it said: "Private Property of Carole N. Shelton. Keep out!"

Carole N.

Like "Carolyn," thought Lizzie, as in "Carolyn Keene," the famous Nancy Drew author? *Interesting.*

Lizzie flipped open the notebook. Carole was using hers as a detective casebook, too. She had lists of suspects and clues and motives.

The lists were exactly like Lizzie's.

"Lizzie, we've gotta go," Miranda whispered. *"Now!"*

But Lizzie couldn't believe what she saw next.

It was the first draft of Carole's mystery story for class.

The Case of the Nasty Notes!

What's going on here? thought Lizzie.

Suddenly, Lizzie felt a sharp tap on her shoulder.

"Excuse me," a voice said. "What *exactly* do you think you're doing?"

It was Carole!

Stay calm—don't panic, Lizzie told herself.

She stood up quickly. For once she didn't hit her head on a locker door. "FYI," she told Carole. "I'm solving a mystery."

Carole glared at her and crossed her arms. "So, it's true what everyone is saying about you, Lizzie McGuire."

"Oh, yeah?" Miranda said. "And what is that?"

"Yeah," Gordo echoed. He looked ready to go into his martial arts pose again. "What is that?"

Carole shrugged. "She's a terrible person. Look,

she was going through my private, personal stuff. You are so busted, Lizzie."

"Maybe," Lizzie said. "But you're *double*-busted, Carole *N*." She held up a pad of yellow sticky notes. And Carole's English notebook.

Carole looked really nervous. "G-give me that," she said. "Right now."

"No," Lizzie said. "Not until you start talking."

"I'm taking the Fifth," Carole said. "That means I have the right to remain silent."

"I *know* what it means," Lizzie said.

"You can't prove anything," Carole said stubbornly.

"On the contrary, my dear Watson," Lizzie said. "I mean, *Carole*," she corrected quickly. "I have all the evidence I need."

That wasn't totally true. But she did have a lot of proof so far. All she really needed now was a confession.

It was worth a try.

"So, why did you send everyone all those mean notes?" Lizzie said. "And why were you trying to make me look bad? Do you totally hate me?"

To Lizzie's surprise, Carole's face suddenly crumpled. "No," she said. "I don't hate you. I wish I was more like you. That's the problem."

Lizzie stared at her. "Say *what*?"

Carole's eyes filled with tears. "I mean, you read all those Nancy Drew books. And you solved the mystery of Kate's missing teddy bear."

This is not making sense, Lizzie thought. "*Um*, Carole," she said. "That was, like, *years* ago."

Carole began to sob.

Lizzie looked at Miranda and Gordo. Her friends seemed totally stunned.

"Hey, listen, guys," Lizzie told them. "Maybe Carole and I need to talk for a while. Alone."

"Right," Gordo said. He looked at Miranda. "We were . . . just leaving. Science."

Miranda nodded. "We're outie," she said. "And don't worry about being late. I'll tell the teacher you're busy helping Carole out with something."

Lizzie nodded her thanks, and watched Miranda and Gordo beat it down the hall.

Carole gave a big sniff. Lizzie handed her a napkin from her jeans jacket pocket. It said "Digital Bean."

When Carole saw it, she started to cry again.

Lizzie put an arm around the girl's shoulders.

Yikes! i can't believe i'm actually doing this. Real detectives aren't supposed to try to make the perps feel better!

"I'm really sorry, Lizzie," Carole said. She blew her nose loudly. "It's just that I'm under so much pressure. It's totally hard, sometimes, being the daughter of a professional mystery writer."

"Oh, yeah," Lizzie said. "Sure."

Lizzie was suddenly glad her own mom was *normal*.

"I know Mother wants me to be a writer, too," Carole went on. "She's always talking about how her big mystery-writing idol, Mary Higgins Clark, must be so proud to watch her daughter follow in her footsteps." Carole sniffled again. "You know, Carol Higgins Clark?"

"Um, right," Lizzie said.

"So, when Ms. George told us she'd pick the best mystery story in the class to be published, and Miranda was talking about how you solved that mystery with Mr. Fuzzy Wuzzy—"

"Wugglesby," Lizzie broke in. "Mr. Stewart Wugglesby."

"—Well, that made me think you would be

perfect to play my detective character," Carole finished.

"Carole," Lizzie said. "That was *grade school.*"

"Just bear with me here," Carole said. "I'm trying to explain."

Lizzie looked up at the clock above the drinking fountain. She and Carole were now officially late for class.

She hoped Miranda was doing a decent job covering for them.

Oh, well. When you've already got two weeks of detention, what's another few more fun-filled days?

"Mother is always telling me how the best fiction is based on fact," Carole went on. "You know, how stories should be as true to life as possible."

"So, you decided to play out a story for real with *me* as the main character," Lizzie said. "And then you planned to write everything as it happened. Is that what you're telling me?"

"Yes," Carole said in a small voice.

"Aaargh!" Lizzie clapped both hands to her head. This was totally nuts!

"Lizzie, you have to believe me," Carole said. "I was going to reveal the truth about those notes in the end."

"Oh, yeah?" Lizzie asked.

Carole nodded. "I thought getting the whole school involved in my story would make people want to read it even more when it got published in *Chief Suspect Junior* magazine." She hung her head. "I didn't actually want you to take the blame in the end."

Lizzie bit her lip. Am I supposed to believe all this? she wondered. She had to admit, she felt really sorry for Carole. It probably *was* hard having a mom with expectations like that.

And one thing was certain. *No one*—not even Carole's mom herself—could make up such a crazy story.

"Please forgive me, Lizzie," Carole begged. "I'm really, really sorry."

Hey, she caused me a whole lot of trouble! And I'm stuck with two weeks of detention! Throw her in the slammer and toss the key!

Lizzie sighed. "Okay, Carole," she said finally. "I guess I understand. As long as you tell everyone the truth, including Principal Tweedy, I'll try to forgive you."

Maybe, she added to herself.

"Oh, thank you, Lizzie!" Carole cried.

"*If* you do my detention time," Lizzie added.

"Deal," Carole said. Her face suddenly brightened. "Hey, I just thought of something," she said. "Now I have an awesome ending for my mystery story!"

"Gee, great," Lizzie said.

There was just one more teeny, tiny problem, Lizzie realized. She'd been so busy solving Carole's mystery, she had never sat down and written her *own* story!

It was due on Monday. *Ugh*. She'd better get cracking.

Hmmm . . . true-to-life stories make the best fiction, huh? How about one starring a famous mystery writer and her way-too-competitive daughter? MOO-HA-HA!

* * *

"So, all's well that ends well," Miranda said to Lizzie at lunch a week later. "Right?"

"Right," Lizzie said. "I guess."

"Hey, Ms. George picked your story *and* Carole's to be published in *Chief Suspect Junior*," Miranda said. "So, you'll be a real, official writer. That's pretty cool."

Lizzie smiled. "It was kind of cool that the contest ended up a tie. Carole said her mom was really happy. Actually, my mom was, too."

"Hey, there, mystery fans," Gordo said, strolling up. "Do I have something to show *you*." He tossed a large, thick envelope onto their table. "It's top secret. *Our* eyes only."

"What is it?" Lizzie asked.

Gordo looked smug. "Only the results of my own private detective investigation," he said. "I think you're going to be impressed. Check it out."

Lizzie tore open the envelope. Half a dozen magazines fell into her lap.

"Parenting mags?" Miranda said. "With all that baby stuff? *Weird.* What's this for?"

"Well," said Gordo, "I walked by Ethan Craft at lunch a few days ago, and I overheard him bragging to a group of girls that he knew all about professional modeling. When the girls asked for more details, he just said his stepmother had helped arrange 'some modeling work' for him a while back—although he refused to say for what."

"So?" asked Lizzie.

"So," continued Gordo, "the night you met him at the Digital Bean, you said his secret had something to do with his 'stepmom' and 'cutesy, baby stuff,' and 'vitamins,' right?"

"Right," said Lizzie.

"So, turn to the pages I marked with the yellow sticky notes," Gordo said.

Lizzie glared at him for using *that* particular method to mark the pages. But she flipped to them, anyway. Each of the pages showed the same advertisement running in the various magazines.

In each of the ads, she recognized Ethan Craft's face staring out at her. He looked totally hot, as usual. Except for one thing—

"He's wearing a baby bonnet," Lizzie said in disbelief.

"Correct-o," Gordo said. "Is that a riot or what? Ethan's stepmom roped him into some modeling contract for Big Baby Vitamins. He had no idea until it was too late. The ad's running in about ten magazines this month."

"So that was the big secret Ethan was trying to tell Lizzie about?" Miranda asked.

"Yep," Gordo said. "So *now* what do you think of the Hillridge hottie?"

Lizzie looked at the ads again. Ethan was sitting in a huge baby carriage, wearing the baby hat and holding a rattle. The print below the picture said: GIVE YOUR CHILD BIG BABY VITAMINS AND WATCH HIM GROW BIGGER AND STRONGER EVERY DAY!

"Poor Ethan," Lizzie said. "He looks totally mortified."

"Well, I think he looks kind of cute," Miranda said.

"Mmmm," Lizzie said. "You're right. Look at that adorable little dimple."

Gordo threw up his hands. "Chicks," he said with a sigh. "Guess we guys will never get a clue."

Want to have a way cool time? Here's a clue. . . . Read the next Lizzie McGuire Mystery!

Case at CAMP GET-ME-OUTIE

Lizzie's parents are sending her to camp. *Science* camp. *Ugh!* Okay, so her crush-boy Ethan is going. And her best friend, Gordo, too—but not because *his* science grades are weak. Gordo's actually *excited* about going. He even enters the camp's Best Invention competition. But when his entry is stolen, he turns to Lizzie for some sleuthing help. Lizzie promises to help Gordo sniff out the suspects and find his invention—and, if she's lucky, maybe he'll find a way to get her outie!

Hello? Do i *want* to spend my summer vacation with flammable elements?